AF451274

After the Badge: My Experiences and Reflections as a Police Officer

David Kujabi

Ukiyoto Publishing

All global publishing rights are held by

Ukiyoto Publishing

Published in 2024

Content Copyright © David Kujabi

ISBN 9789361727252

All rights reserved.
No part of this publication may be reproduced, transmitted, or stored in a retrieval system, in any form by any means, electronic, mechanical, photocopying, recording or otherwise, without the prior permission of the publisher.

The moral rights of the author have been asserted.

This memoir is based on actual life events. While every effort has been made to accurately portray the experiences recounted, some names, characters, businesses, places, events, and incidents have been altered or recreated for narrative clarity or privacy protection. Any resemblance to actual persons, living or deceased, or events is coincidental. The author acknowledges that memory can be subjective and interpretations of events may vary. This work is intended to offer a personal perspective and should not be construed as a comprehensive historical account.This book is sold subject to the condition that it shall not by way of trade or otherwise, be lent, resold, hired out or otherwise circulated, without the publisher's prior consent, in any form of binding or cover other than that in which it is published.

www.ukiyoto.com

Dedicated to all men and women of The Gambia Police Force. I salute you all for your service to the nation.

Contents

The Early School Days in Bwiam

For most Gambians born in the 70s and beyond, their first day of school is a memory they will always hold. This was because the school-going age for most children back then was seven and beyond. I formally enrolled at 7, but I'd been going to school before. My father was a teacher, and my grandfather was Pa Harry Kujabi, a missionary who, along with Irish Catholic priests, planted the seed of Christianity and Western education in Foni.

The church, school, parish house, and my grandfather's house were within the same vicinity. When they came of age, my grandfather's children also built their homes around the same area known in Bwiam as Mission. My father's house was closest to the primary school, about 40 metres from the nearest classroom, Primary One. So, at about the age of 4, my mom would, after feeding me, bathe me, dress me, and ask me to run into the classroom to join my older cousin Tubabo, who was in that very class. I still remember that the class teacher was MB Bojang, a very amiable man (God rest his soul).

I enjoyed going to class and sitting beside my cousin, who had a place in the back of the classroom. My favourite times were after the break when there was storytelling, recitation of rhymes, singing and dancing. I still recall how with joy I would sing the last song after the closure bell rang at 2 p.m. "goodbye, goodbye teacher, our daily school is over, we are going home. We hope to see again…." and will not stop until I got to my mom's welcome embrace at the kitchen veranda. Even though I do not have many recollections of that time, I still feel the happiness I had as an unregistered pupil at St. Edward's Primary School.

The language of communication at home was Jola, but I was in an environment where many other languages were spoken. Mandinka, Wolof, and English were widely spoken. For pupils of class one, a teacher would have to translate into the various languages for the pupils to understand. For most of us, it was difficult to distinguish which language was which and which one we were supposed to learn. For example, when learning the noun UNCLE, to make us understand, the teacher tells us in Jola, it is called *tontong*; in Mandinka, it is *mbaring*; in Fulani, it is *kaw*, and in Wolof, it's called *nijai*. You can imagine how young brains often get it mixed up. In high school, my mom told me about a childhood encounter.

She said I had closed school excited to tell her what I had learned, "you came running looking very excited and calling *'Ena Ena*, I know how to call a thread in English!' and when I asked you how it's called you said *julboro*", she said. Apparently, speaking my mother tongue, Jola, I had given the Mandinka name for thread, thinking it was English. This was and continues to be a challenge for many young Africans who must learn a foreign language and are expected to excel in it. Imagine the challenge we went through learning the language of instruction (English) while also learning Arithmetic, Quantitative, Verbal Aptitude, etc. The cane was not spared to force us to learn, so to survive, we memorised rather than tried to understand.

So, instead of getting educated, we were instructed; instead of being taught to use thought, we were told what to think. Over time, only a few escape this prison of programmed education to become truly educated, and I am still trying to escape that prison.

The Dilemma of Learning English and Getting an Education

Learning colonial languages such as English and French in African educational systems introduces a multifaceted challenge. These languages bring with them intricate grammar rules, complex syntax, precise spelling, and demanding pronunciation, all of which divert valuable cognitive resources away from the core educational content. The process of acquiring these colonial languages often overshadows critical aspects of education, such as critical thinking, creativity, and problem-solving. This linguistic hurdle can hinder genuine comprehension and intellectual development.

Comparatively, learning one's mother tongue is inherently natural and intuitive. Children absorb the nuances of their native language effortlessly through constant exposure and interaction. Concepts are easily grasped, and communication becomes a seamless process. In contrast, colonial languages impose a cognitive load, hindering the natural flow of learning and expression.

Moreover, the colonial legacy extends to educational materials. Missionaries translated religious texts, including the Bible, into various native languages to spread Christianity. However, this effort did not extend to schoolbooks and educational resources. Consequently, African children find themselves caught between two worlds: their rich, expressive native languages and the rigid, often alien structure of colonial languages imposed upon them through the education system.

This linguistic struggle transcends academic performance; it profoundly influences cultural identity. The disconnect between one's cultural heritage and the language of instruction can breed a sense of alienation and erode self-esteem. It creates a psychological divide, making the learning process intimidating and less effective.

In addressing these challenges, a Pan-African perspective emphasizes the importance of recognizing and revitalizing indigenous languages within the educational framework. By embracing native languages as mediums of instruction, African countries not only preserve their cultural legacies but also enhance the overall learning experience. This approach instils a profound sense of pride and belonging, empowering African children to engage more meaningfully with their education and the broader global landscape. Ultimately, it fosters a more inclusive, culturally rich, and self-assured educational environment that aligns with the aspirations of a united and empowered African continent.

I and many other Africans underwent this established education system, and on 12 June 1998, I graduated from Senior Secondary School at eighteen with not-too-impressive exam results. Of the nine subjects I sat in, I earned five credits and one pass. I failed Maths and Biology. As a matter of fact, I've consistently failed Maths.

I was not a bad student, but I could have taken my academic work seriously. I skipped class frequently, especially Maths periods and did not study much. I am a fast learner, but I forget quickly. Therefore, I always wait until exam timetables are out before studying. Of course, I needed more time to read all the notes on the various subjects, so I only chose topics to read and hoped for the best. This often worked out for me, although it never put me amongst the best three students in the class. I often fell between the fourth and tenth positions and was perfectly okay with that.

My batch of students was what I describe as guinea pigs of the Gambia education system. When I got to Primary Six in September 1991, the Government of the Gambia was changing the education system. We were the first students not to sit the Common Entrance Examination. We started what was then called the Primary School Leaving Certificate Examination (PSLCE). Instead of sitting exams to get into secondary school or high school, we were prepared to go into Grade 7. As a new system, there was no teacher reference point, so we were made to work extra hard to prepare for the unknown. Again, we were the first to sit for the Grade 9 and Grade 12 exams.

I may not have been too serious with my academic work, but I was an avid reader of novels. I developed a passion for reading in primary school, which grew more throughout the years up to my undergraduate studies. Whenever I picked up an exciting book, I often became so engrossed that I read all day and night. Sometimes, even during class, I would put the book on my lap under the table and read while lessons were being taught. My reading helped shape my liberal and analytical mind. It was my little escape from the chains of spoon-fed education.

In 1998, high school graduates had a few options to further their education. The tertiary institutions available were mainly The Gambian College and Gambia Technical Training Institute (GTTI). That same year, university education was introduced through the St. Mary's University Extension Program for the first time. For many Gambians, the easiest way to gain employment was to enlist in the army, police, or any other security force or become a teacher. Coming from a family of teachers, my obvious option was to become a teacher.

Nurturing Minds and Shaping Futures: My Journey as a Teacher

In September 1998, I embarked on my journey as an untrained teacher at St. Peter's Primary School in Lamin. My assignment was to teach Primary 3, and from the very beginning, I developed a strong bond with my young students. Despite being just eighteen years old, my passion for teaching burned brightly, and I was eager to explore my full potential. While I admired colleagues who ventured abroad, I remained grounded in reality, understanding that my means did not allow such dreams. Instead, I patiently awaited the opportunity many Gambians pursued – college enrollment.

The summer of 1999 brought the Primary Teachers Certificate (PTC) entrance exams, consisting of three challenging papers: English, Mathematics, and General Knowledge. It was apparent that I hadn't met the passing threshold, particularly in mathematics. Undaunted, I returned to teaching as an untrained educator but with a new assignment at St. Edward's Primary School in Bwiam, my hometown. Here, I took on the role of teaching Primary 4, one grade higher than my previous class.

In 2000, I applied for the Higher Teachers Certificate (HTC) program, enrolling to study English Language and Agricultural Science. This move marked another transition, as the college extended the program from two to three years that year. Previously, it was a two-year program comprising one term of teaching practice. The shift now entailed two years of academic studies and one year of practical teaching experience.

My college life, particularly campus life, was an intriguing chapter. Despite maintaining good grades, my approach to academics remained consistent – I aimed for excellence. Still, I didn't chase the title of the best student. I continued to immerse myself in novels and the world around me, forging numerous friendships and acquaintances from whom I drew invaluable life lessons. My days at Gambia College still evoke cherished memories and stand as the highlight of my student life.

In September 2003, I became a qualified teacher and was posted to St. Martin's Basic Cycle School. This was a significant moment as it was the same school where I had completed my Primary education from grades 3 to 6. It felt like a homecoming of sorts. During my tenure there, I received distressing news – my high school sweetheart, now in the United States, had married another. Heartbroken and devastated, I initially sought solace in alcohol but soon realized it was a futile escape from my pain. Determined to channel my emotions constructively, I turned to writing. At the age of twenty-four, I made a personal commitment to publish a book by my twenty-fifth birthday. This was the genesis of my book "The Chain and The Amulet," which, though completed in 2005, remained unpublished until 2024.

In 2008, during my final year at the University of The Gambia (UTG), I took on a part-time teaching role at St. Peter's High School. My responsibilities included instructing Grade 8, Grade 10, and Grade 12 students. Remarkably, the Grade 12 class comprised mostly of students I had taught in Grade 3 in 1998. This was an extraordinary experience, as I had witnessed their growth from novice learners to the culmination of their Senior Secondary School education. For me, this marked a profound achievement – I had not just taught lessons but had played a part in shaping a generation.

Becoming a Police Officer

In July 2009, I completed University with a major in English Language and a minor in Sociology. Reflecting on my time as a student at the University of The Gambia (UTG), my journey unfolded smoothly despite various challenges. During my university years, I was employed as a teacher on study leave, receiving a qualified teacher's salary. Additionally, I was fortunate to secure a half scholarship from the Nova-Scotia Gambia Association (NSGA), with the other half graciously provided by my Senior Secondary School English Language teacher and mentor, Mr. Diarmete Roache, whose memory I hold dear.

One peculiar aspect of being a UTG student was the absence of a traditional campus. Instead, classes were scattered across various locations, from the Management Development Institute (MDI) to the faculty building at the end of MDI road, the Young Men's Christian Association (YMCA) building, Alliance Franco-Gambienne, and even the School of Nursing in Banjul. My friend Andrew Jassey humorously referred to us as "nomadic" students due to our constant relocation.

At Gambia College, I pursued English Language as a major, a choice I made at UTG for my bachelor's degree. While this knowledge significantly contributed to my professional growth, I later lamented not opting for a more specialised field like political science, development studies, or economics. Upon completing my bachelor's degree, I found myself compelled to return to teaching, realising that an English language degree in the Gambian job market limited my prospects primarily to academia.

In September 2009, I assumed the role of Vice Principal II at St. Theresa's Upper Basic School. Although the appointment felt overwhelming for someone my age and experience, I embraced the challenge wholeheartedly. It marked the commencement of my practical leadership journey.

As Vice Principal, my responsibilities included internal administration and student discipline. Despite initial doubts from sceptics, I excelled in my role. However, despite the comfortable salary, I couldn't shake off a growing discontent with the school environment. My father spent his entire career and my childhood within school compounds added to my sense of restlessness. The adventurous spirit within me yearned for a new experience, prompting me to scour newspapers for job vacancies.

One fateful day, while perusing a newspaper, I stumbled upon an advertisement seeking applications from university and college graduates to enlist as Cadet Police Officers. The idea of becoming a police officer had never crossed my mind. Still, the prospect of a fresh start proved irresistible. Without much hesitation, I submitted my application.

A few weeks later, I received a call from the police headquarters inviting me for a job interview. Despite initial apprehension and thoughts of withdrawing, I mustered the courage to attend. The interview was scheduled for a Saturday morning in Banjul.

Upon arrival at the impressive police headquarters, I was surprised to encounter familiar faces, fellow university colleagues like Lazar Kujabi, Abdou Bojang, Lamin Jaiteh, Omar D. Bah, and others. Their presence helped ease my nervousness and apprehension. However, after a considerable wait, we were informed that the interviews would be postponed due to emergencies requiring the Inspector General of Police's attention. Disappointed but undeterred, we returned the following day.

The second day arrived, but Lazar Kujabi was notably absent, leaving me to wonder if he had reconsidered. We were instructed to wait in a corridor on the top floor while interview panel members prepared. Engaging in conversation, we aimed to alleviate the tension surrounding us. Finally, a group of officials, led by the petite-looking middle-aged Inspector General of Police, Yankuba JN Sonko, ascended the stairs. I recognised Mr Abdoulie Sanyang, my Grade 7 teacher at Fatima Junior Secondary School in 1993. He taught social and environmental studies during his teaching trainee days at The Gambia College. Their warm yet serious demeanour set the tone for the impending interviews, and candidates were called in individually.

When my turn arrived, I entered the interview room, greeted the all-male panel, and awaited their instructions. While I can't recall all the questions, one stood out: "What motivated you to join the police?" This question caught me off guard, as I lacked concrete motivation. In truth, I wasn't entirely sure I wanted to be there. Still, I admitted as much, saying, "I have no specific motivation per se. I saw the job advertisement and thought I could apply for something new." The interview continued with more questions, to which I provided my best responses. Ultimately, I was dismissed, with the promise that they would contact me.

Approximately a week later, I received a call from the police headquarters informing me to collect my appointment letter as a Cadet Assistant Superintendent of Police (C/ASP). Although I did not know its significance, the long title sounded impressive. This career move necessitated my resignation from the position of Vice Principal, a decision met with disapproval, including from my father. While he didn't oppose my choice, he harboured reservations, reflecting the sentiment that none of his immediate family members had ventured into the security sector. He said, "Your grandfather did not want any of his children to join the police because he thought they were no good." It was only years later that I fully grasped my grandfather's perspective. Despite the mixed reactions, I remained uncertain about my decision. Still, I committed to exploring a different path, with policing as my chosen journey.

A few days before officially reporting to the Police Training School for basic recruitment training, Inspector General of Police Mr Yankuba JN Sonko summoned us to the police headquarters. He dedicated considerable time to mentally preparing us for the challenges ahead. He shared his experiences as a cadet officer in both Gambia and Nigeria, emphasising that as graduates, we would face harassment, undeserved punishment, and deliberate humiliation by our instructors. He encouraged us to stand firm, recognising that this training process would instil a spirit of service in us. From that moment, I greatly admired IGP Sonko, viewing him as an exceptional leader and a fatherly figure. His simplicity, humility, and down-to-earth nature revealed a man with a vision for the Gambia Police Force, and my respect for him has remained unwavering. He is one of the most outstanding leaders I've ever had the privilege to work under.

Baptism and Commencement of Police Training

On June 1, 2010, a group of ten individuals embarked on a transformative journey as we boarded a bus bound for the Police Training School in Yundum. Within our group, seven of us held the rank of Cadet ASPs, while the remaining three were designated Cadet Inspectors. Our arrival coincided with the lunch hour, and the reception we encountered was every bit as chilly as we had been forewarned.

Upon reaching the training school, we were granted a brief respite to organise our belongings before being provided with a meal. Following this initial meal, a significant change awaited us – our heads were to be cleanly shaven, leaving us with the distinctive appearance of bald heads. Just as we completed this transformation, the shrill blast of a whistle reverberated through the air, accompanied by the commanding cry of "Fall in …!" All around us, recruits abruptly abandoned their activities, converging swiftly and in a disciplined manner on an open area within the campus grounds.

Initially, we remained unsure of what to do until a booming voice jolted us out of our confusion. "Cadets! Fall in!" we were ordered. Swiftly, we got up and hastened to the designated area, where some instructors directed us where to stand. Marching to the centre of the ground, a tall, slender, and impeccably dressed police officer halted and loudly issued what sounded like "Pred, pred shun!" All the recruits executed some movements and stood at attention while we stood perplexed. "Cadets as you were!" the officer barked at us. Consequently, we all reverted to the attention position somewhat disorganised.

"I am RSM Jobe, and this is my 'holy ground,'" he declared, pointing to the ground we stood on. "When you are on it, you do as I command!" he exclaimed again. In response, the recruits echoed, "Sir, Yes, Sir," while we observed, still bewildered. "Oh, so you Cadet Officers think you are too big to respond to me, eh? Just wait until I am done baptising you!" he warned with a menacing glare. He then instructed the recruits to fetch water for our "baptism." We were instructed to lie flat on the ground, and buckets of water were poured over us as we were directed to roll over in the wet soil. This ceremony was accompanied by chanting, jeering, and laughter from the other recruits, who continued to drench us.

After what felt like an eternity, we were permitted to stand up. As the dizziness faded, RSM Jobe called us to attention again. He pointed to two trees at opposite ends of the ground and instructed us to run back and forth between them several times. We did so, occasionally colliding with each other, but we dared not stop. Realising that some of us were nearing exhaustion and a few were on the verge of passing out, RSM Jobe halted the exercise. He then divided us into two groups, placing us at opposite ends, with one group required to shout "Sir Yes Sir" while the other responded likewise. This continued for several minutes, during which I grew fatigued and short of breath, wondering, "What on earth have we gotten ourselves into?"

Our relief finally arrived when Superintendent Lamin Banda, the Deputy Commandant of the Training School, intervened and informed RSM Jobe that it was sufficient. Drenched, muddy, and gasping for breath, we were lined up, and Commissioner Mamour Jobe, the school's Commandant, formally welcomed us. After his address, he suggested we take a group photo, considering it a memorable keepsake. He then directed that we be allowed to shower and settle in, as training would commence the following morning.

Pairs were formed, and we were assigned to various rooms within the camp. I shared a room and bed with Demba S. Jammeh, which happened to be a double-decked bed, with one mattress on top and another below. Opting for the upper bunk, I was fortunate to have it near a window, affording me some respite from the heat. Our room, named "Nimba 3," accommodated eight other recruits. As a Cadet ASP and the most senior, I naturally assumed a leadership role within our room.

After we had taken our showers and settled into our respective accommodations, the piercing sound of a whistle summoned us for dinner. At that moment, exhaustion weighed heavily upon me, and all I yearned for was a good night's rest. However, some of my fellow recruits wisely encouraged me to partake in the evening meal, emphasising the importance of replenishing our energy for the challenges that lay ahead.

With that advice in mind, I retrieved the plate that had been provided to me earlier as part of our supplies and joined the line in the kitchen to receive my dinner. Although you may be curious about the specifics of the meal, I'll leave that detail aside for now, except to say that it was surprisingly palatable. After dinner, I returned to my sleeping quarters while others dispersed to various activities.

Some recruits utilised the classroom for additional studying, while others congregated in the campus yard, diligently practising their drill and marching skills. Some gathered to brew *ataya* and engage in lively conversations. As for myself, I climbed onto my modest bed. I can assure you that I prayed fervently to my Maker that night as I attempted to sleep with one eye and ear alert, as we had been advised. Despite the advantageous placement of my bed near the window and the fatigue lingering from the strenuous baptismal exercise earlier in the day, I must admit that achieving restful sleep proved challenging.

The shrill, persistent sound of a whistle pierced the air, jolting me awake from a half-slumber. It echoed through the dormitory and was swiftly followed by a voice exclaiming *"fitique, fitique."* Amid this sudden commotion, I could hear my fellow recruits hurriedly leaping from their beds, grumbling and uttering a myriad of curses.

With the same urgency, I flung myself out of my bed, narrowly avoiding a collision with Demba, who was also grappling to rise from his own. In my haste, I momentarily forgot that my sleeping quarters were about one and a half meters above the ground. I landed with a resounding thud, nearly twisting my leg.

Glancing at the time, I noted that it was a mere 4:30 a.m. Confused and disoriented, I inquired about the reason for this early disturbance. To my bewilderment, I was informed it was time for *"fitique."* I couldn't help but ask, "What does that mean?" It turned out that *"fitique"* translated to "sweeping." To this day, the origins of that peculiar word elude me. However, it suddenly became clear why we had been instructed to bring brooms. Without hesitation, I retrieved my broom from its resting place beneath Demba's bed. I ventured out of the dormitory to join the rest of the recruits in sweeping the school compound.

One hundred and fifty recruits were divided into four platoons, each with their designated cleaning duties. While this division of labour seemed reasonable, the requirement to sweep and water the gravel road stretching from the training school gate to the main highway has perplexed and puzzled me. This road spanned approximately 300 meters and demanded daily cleaning. The additional, seemingly unnecessary step of watering the road further confounded me. I couldn't fathom the rationale behind these tasks – whether they were part of a socialisation process or merely routine chores. The huge amount of water wasted in this endeavour could have been used for more productive purposes, such as cultivating a banana orchard or tending to a vegetable garden. Nevertheless, I refrained from voicing my questions, recognising my status as a newcomer in this regimented environment.

After completing the morning ritual of sweeping and watering, there was no respite to return to our beds; our day had to commence. By 7:00 a.m., we had all undergone our morning showers and adorned ourselves in our distinctive attire – marching blue baggy shorts and white T-shirts, curiously referred to as *"banyan"*, a term whose origin still baffles me.

Amidst the hustle and bustle of preparing for the day, breakfast was served, but it was far from a leisurely affair. A thunderous voice bellowing abruptly shattered the tranquillity of the meal, *"Keep still! Keep still!"*. Spoons, teacups, and bread were put down, and munching ceased, and all stood at attention as Commissioner Mamour Jobe, Commandant of the Training School, drove into the school compound. It seemed as if the world stopped as the Boss came in. At my own attention position with breathing evenly coordinated and made subtly. In that solemn moment, I couldn't help but contemplate the frequency with which I had assumed such unwavering attention, akin to a sacred ritual. In a hushed tone, I murmured, "This feels like another rite of passage, akin to a traditional circumcision initiation for us".

By 8:00 a.m., all the Cadet Officers were lined up for our first drill lessons. Our drill instructor arrived and commanded, "Cadet Officers, come to attention!" We responded, albeit somewhat disorganised. "As you were! Stand at ease!" he directed, and we attempted again, this time with better coordination. The actual command words were "Parade Attention" and "Stand at ease," but for ease of command, they were pronounced as *"pred pred shun"*.

"By the left, quick march! Left, right, left, right, left..." the instructor commanded, and we marched as best as we could, heading toward the drill ground. I couldn't help but smile, thinking how easy it seemed. I had marched during Independence Day celebrations in primary school, which was always enjoyable. My colleagues appeared to share in the sentiment.

The group of Cadet ASPs included Abdou Bojang, Momodou Kujabi, Lamin Manka, Muhammed Lamin Sonko, Omar D Bah, Lamin Jaiteh, and myself. The Cadet Inspectors comprised Lamin Njie, Malang Jarjou, Demba S Jammeh, and Fatoumatta Touray. Fatoumatta was the sole woman among us; I must admit she was as strong as any of the men. In hindsight, some men persevered through the gruelling training out of fear of ridicule, especially as she met every challenge head-on. Fatoumatta was resilient, strikingly beautiful, and well-endowed. I often teased her about being a welcome distraction, especially when we marched behind her—a frequent occurrence due to her height.

Fatoumatta's status as the sole female in our group of twelve male Cadet Officers was emblematic of the gender imbalance prevalent in the security sector, particularly in senior positions. At that time, there were only a few senior female police officers in the force, including Commissioner Aminata Ndure, Assistant Commissioner of Police (ACP) Amie Nyassi, ACP Lala Camara, Superintendent (Supt.) Marie Gomez, Supt. Ramou Sambou, Assistant Superintendent of Police (ASP) Elizabeth Harding, ASP Marie Ceesay, ASP Fanny Williams, ASP Jankey Saidy, and others. Not more than fifteen female officers were within the officers' core of the Gambia Police Force fifty years after enlisting the first batch of seven female police officers in 1960.

Initially established in 1855 as The Gambia River Police, it took 105 years for the first batch of seven female recruits to be enlisted. Cecilia

Tabbal Senghore, with regiment number 128, is credited as the first of the seven females to join the Gambia Police Force. The duties of these female officers primarily involved arresting female offenders and performing secretarial or clerical work. However, significant improvements have been made, with more female officers holding leadership and senior-level positions. In 2022, Sirreh Jabang was appointed Commissioner of Operations, Gas Shabally became the Operations Commander for Bundung, and Binta Njie was appointed the first Police Public Relations Officer (PRO).

At the parade ground, we started our first drill lessons, attention by numbers, marching, saluting by numbers, about turn by numbers and so on. While doing the actions, we were expected to count aloud as well. It was not easy, and before long, I was tired of the counting and repetition of the counting. The sun was scorching hot, and the upper skins of our bald heads were peeling off from the intense heat. Our voices were going down by the minute, and we were being shouted at "louder, louder". At that moment, I missed my office and the students at St. Therese's. My mind momentarily drifted away, but I was jolted out of my reverie by the instructor, "Cadet as you were! Do you think this is a party ground? Once you are here, you throw your degree away and take commands from me, okay?". Yes, I responded, "As you were! What did you say?" "Sir, Yes Sir", I quickly corrected myself.

We had arrived at the training school two months after the recruits, and since we were at different levels in the drill, the instructors wanted us to move fast to catch up with them. So, we were pushed to almost our tether end, but we hung in there, and as the days went by, we began to appreciate and enjoy the drill. Our instructors were firm but friendly and often understanding and supportive. It was first the foot drill, then the weapons drill and then the riot drill. We learned all under the scorching sun, and the foreskin on our shaven heads peeled off from the intense heat on it.

Our instructors did their best to instruct us despite the lack of a proper training environment and equipment. The training school was, in fact, the female dormitories of the old Yundum College. The facilities there were not designed for police training. The place was small, and even the drills were carried out at the Banjulinding football field. It was more like a makeshift training ground, which the police were compelled to use after establishing the Gambia Gendarmerie. The Fajara Barracks was the traditional training ground for the police. However, police training was moved to Yundum to make room for the Gendarmerie training program which had both policing and military aspects.

The facilities were not only not ideal, but there were also huge challenges in providing proper and adequate training resources. The blue baggy shorts sewn with elastic to hold the waist and poor-quality white T-shirts we wore made us look more like prisoners rather than police trainees. During our weapons training, a few AK 47 rifles were at the instructors' disposal to train more than a hundred recruits. We used woven reeds as shields and sticks as batons for our riot drill. Despite these challenges, the Gambia Police Training School has produced very professional training with an international reputation.

I still hold all our instructors in high esteem; there were Chief Inspectors Demba Baldeh, Yarbo and Touray and Sergeant Badjie. There were the younger ones, Regimental Sergeant Major (RSM) Jobe, Disciplinary Officer (DO) Jobe, Sergeant Momodou Faye, D Jammeh, Sub Inspector (SI) Ansumana Sanyang and two very formidable ladies, Jainaba Sambou, and Maimuna Sanneh all under the watchful eyes of ASP Gallo Sowe who was coordinator of the drill. There were the nice and not the too nice, but they all did what they had to train us into police officers.

ASP Gallo Sowe, of blessed memory, was an enigma; he received no conventional education but was a fine police instructor. He was always neat, impeccably dressed, punctual and highly disciplined. He was non-compromising of standards and would often boast, "Na British train me" (the British trained me). He often told me, "David, *you na woman, you na office material*". The reason was that I smiled a lot, and for him, a police officer must always look serious.

Life at the training school was full of intriguing and interesting experiences, but unfortunately, not all can be told. Besides the physical training, we also received theoretical lessons on policing, criminal and traffic codes, etc. There was a lot to learn, and I realised then that contrary to what most believed, policing was more about using the brain than physical strength. I later concluded that the standards and requirements for recruitment into most police services in Africa, especially former British colonies, were the same for similar reasons. The British were ruling people who resent colonisation and would often rebel against them.

The police force was created to maintain British order and control, and to do that, they needed strong and able-bodied men. The focus was mainly on height and physical fitness and not on education. It was common to hear servicemen say, *"Education no matter"*. However, many smart and well-educated men joined the force despite this fact. The responsibility of the police then was not just to protect life and property but to protect the interests of the colonial masters. For obvious reasons, the police were then viewed as wicked, and that belief has been handed down from generation to generation. This made many people afraid and weary of police officers, not out of some bad experience but out of the stereotype handed down to them.

My training made me realise that police are meant to protect life and property, maintain law and order, and not intimidate or harass anyone. This understanding not only made me appreciate the work of police but also made me eager to go out and serve. However, as I grew in experience and knowledge, I realised that despite the reoriented focus of policing in providing a service of law enforcement in conformity with respect for fundamental human rights, the training was still shaped to serve the master and not really the people.

Training as a Cadet Police Officer

RSM Jobe possessed an uncanny knack for discipline, frequently singling out us, the Cadet Officers, for his reprimands. During our breaks from rigorous drills, he'd summon us, remarking, "Cadets, it's hot today." We'd agree, only for him to retort, "Alright, then, go and bathe." In the scorching afternoons, he subjected us to showers, fully clothed, and heaven help anyone who didn't get thoroughly soaked.

However, my most vivid recollection from the training school involved an incident where we were made to frog-jump approximately 100 meters. It was a punishment doled out because one of the recruits had erred, and RSM insisted that, as a team, we must all bear the consequences. "One man does all pay the price," he proclaimed. I didn't take issue with collective punishment as it instilled camaraderie, but I bristled at the thought of being penalised without reason. The memory of us frog-jumping aimlessly remains etched in my mind. I was not just upset; I was incensed by what I perceived as inhumane treatment. At that juncture, the thought of walking away crossed my mind, but I resisted, fearing the label of cowardice it would attach to me. RSM Jobe excelled at his role, breaking us down and moulding us into what he believed were disciplined officers.

Our batch of Cadet Officers was not the first, but we were the largest group ever recruited simultaneously. Many officers in the police ranks frowned upon the idea of admitting so many young graduates into the force. In contrast, I believed they lacked the vision of IGP Sonko. He seemed acutely aware of the challenges the country faced under President Jammeh's rule, and he aimed to lay the foundation for a stronger police force in the future. To guide us on this path, he affectionately referred to us as his cadets and closely monitored our progress. He frequently visited us at the training school, both during working hours and off-duty, offering encouragement. Even after our batch, IGP Sonko continued to recruit more graduates into the police force. Thanks to his foresight, by 2018, the GPF had enlisted over 129 university graduates from diverse fields, including five medical doctors. He also championed scholarships for serving police officers to further their education. In contrast to the colonial adage "education no matter," he made education matter.

Our Training School's Commandant, Commissioner Mamour Jobe, was an excellent mentor. He kept us engaged both on and off the drill field. He encouraged Cadet Officers to develop their public speaking skills by taking turns addressing the morning parade. We watched GRTS news, took notes, and presented our own versions on the parade ground. Despite its difficulty, we put forth our best efforts, and our dedication earned commendations from all quarters.

One day, while on break, I received a summons to Commissioner Jobe's office. I promptly complied, stood at his office door, and greeted, "Good afternoon, Sir." "Good afternoon, come on in, David," he replied. Stepping into his office, I noticed certificates and photos adorning the walls, chronicling his illustrious career as a police officer.

While at attention, he presented me with a stack of handouts, describing them as notes on policing. He entrusted me with reviewing them, cross-referencing them with our police training manual, and creating a more comprehensive version. He suggested recruits competent at typing, like Awa SO Jobe and Baboucarr Jeng, to assist me. As I exited his office with the stack of handouts, I couldn't help but wonder why he had chosen me among equally or more competent colleagues.

Regardless of the rationale, I resolved not to disappoint him. In the ensuing days, I meticulously studied all the handouts, devising the best approach to compile them, using the old manual as a reference. With the assistance of recruits Awa SO Jobe and Baboucarr Jeng, I embarked on this demanding task. It granted me a valid excuse to exempt myself from sweeping, watering, and road running, allowing me to gain deeper insights into the theoretical aspects of policing.

Our training progressed smoothly, and we acclimated to the system. Though Lamin Manka often fell ill, he persevered and emerged as a highly respected police officer. Manka consistently followed the rulebook, earning him the reputation of a dependable officer. Among us, Lamin Njie stood out as the most physically robust. He was proficient both in the field and in the classroom and had an excellent sense of humour. We developed a close friendship and frequently spent late nights engaged in conversation. In 2011, Abdou Bojang, Lamin Njie, and I collaborated to launch the POLISO magazine, which became a household name in The Gambia. Njie and I continued working in the Press Office, where he succeeded me as the Public Relations Officer in 2015, following my departure for a peacekeeping mission in Darfur.

Muhammed Lamin Sonko was the chattiest among us, never missing an opportunity to remind us that he had served as a Regional Education Officer before joining the police. Sonko later became my roommate during our cadet course at the Ghana Police College. He'd have my head if I shared some of our experiences there. Nevertheless, he was a supportive brother who consistently offered wise counsel, even if I didn't always heed it. I still hold him dear. Lamin Jaiteh exuded eagerness, striving to be the first in almost everything. He often garnered teasing for marching ahead even before the command was given.

Abdou Bojang was the quietest of our group, but our conversations were always mentally stimulating. He might appear unassuming, but his intelligence and sense of humour were remarkable. He possessed wisdom, and every chat with him offered valuable insights. The rest of the group each brought unique qualities to the police force, affirming that IGP Sonko and his team made no mistakes in selecting us.

After three months of intensive basic recruitment training, we celebrated our graduation in a grand ceremony presided over by the then Minister of Interior, Ousman Sonko. I didn't participate in the march but had the honour of reciting a poem during the event. Following this, we embarked on another three-month endeavour, the Cadet Officers Course. This course aimed to prepare us for our roles as middle managers within the force. It concluded successfully, equipping us with much theoretical knowledge about policing.

As Cadet Officers, we remained on probation, with the next phase involving Cadet Officer Rotation. This program mandated a three-year probationary period, during which we rotated every three months among different units within the police force. These units encompassed the charge office, traffic, Criminal Investigations Department (CID), Crime Records Office (CRO), INTERPOL,

Criminal Investigations Unit (CIU), and more. The objective was to provide Cadet Officers with a comprehensive understanding of all police units.

My cadet rotation commenced at the police headquarters, where I served as an administrative officer to the Commissioner of Administration. To my surprise, my supervisor was none other than my former Grade 7 teacher, Mr. Abdoulie Sanyang. My duties involved handling internal and external correspondence, recording minutes during Senior Management Meetings, and organising documents, among other tasks. While the role proved relatively straightforward for me, I faced a dilemma. After a few months, the consequences of leaving a well-paying job for one with meagre earnings began to weigh on me. My salary was so paltry that it barely covered my rent, let alone my other expenses. I often arrived at work with empty pockets, unable to afford breakfast. The office supplied tea, coffee, and sugar but little else. During this period, I often subsisted on multiple cups of coffee, perpetually hungry yet masquerading as content.

Commute posed another challenge, as police officers were not provided transportation at the time. It was common to see officers hitchhiking rides to and from work. My pride and fear of judgment prevented me from stooping to this level. Instead, I woke up at 5 a.m. to catch a prison services truck to Banjul. Unfortunately, it only took me as far as Mile 2, leaving a significant distance to cover before reaching the police headquarters.

Observing my struggles, Solomon Kujabi, a cousin who worked at the Gambia Ports Authority (GPA), arranged for me to join their staff bus to Banjul. While this was a welcome solution, the bus departed early, resulting in my arrival in Banjul well before 6 a.m., when the offices were not open, and the streets remained deserted. To pass the time, I often attended morning mass at the cathedral, arriving long before the service began. Unwittingly, I found myself compelled to pray to occupy the hours. I persevered and drew strength from my experiences, likening myself to rams preparing for a fierce clash, retreating briefly to gather strength for the ultimate confrontation.

Eventually, the police command acquired buses for staff transportation. I resided in Lamin, and the nearest bus followed a route from Brikama to Banjul via the Coastal Road. I had to rise early and walk about three kilometres from Lamin to the airport junction to catch it. I recall one day when I was slightly late and witnessed the bus departing. As usual, I lacked the funds for the fare. Dressed in my white uniform, I felt embarrassed to linger around, awaiting a ride. In a bold move, I removed my uniform, stashed it in my bag, and walked back home in just a singlet, pretending to embark on a morning stroll. Meanwhile, my colleagues told me about their rotations in various units and police stations nationwide. I, too, longed to move on, but my commissioner initially resisted, refusing to release me even after three months. I persisted, asserting my need for experience, and my determination finally paid off. I secured my rotation and was posted to Brusubi Police Station.

I relished my work at Brusubi Station under the leadership of the kind and generous MI Joof. My days were primarily spent at the charge office counter, observing police officers receive complaints, logging them in the diary, conducting interviews, and taking appropriate actions. I found this process truly fascinating. I still hold fond memories of some of the officers. Unfortunately, my tenure at Brusubi lasted only three weeks before I was recalled to headquarters. Permission had been granted to launch a police magazine, and I was tasked with overseeing its production. While I excitedly departed Brusubi, I regretted that my time there had been so short. That marked the end of my Cadet Rotation.

Over time, I've realised that the layout of our police stations is far from user-friendly. It offers minimal privacy and can be quite intimidating. The charge office counter, in particular, is an uncomfortable barrier, making it challenging for victims of sensitive cases to report their concerns. Additionally, detention centres are often located within the charge office, requiring anyone entering the police station to explain their issues in the presence of everyone, including detained suspects.

I've also observed that policing in The Gambia tends to be relatively uncomplicated. This could be attributed to Gambians' strong adherence to the law, their respect for the police, or perhaps a genuine fear of them. Often, when a complainant reports a case at a police station, the duty officer would record the details in the station diary, including the date, time, and complainant. They'd then inquire if the complainant had identified a suspect and, if so, request their contact information. Surprisingly, the suspects would often voluntarily report to the police station to address the complaints against them.

One traditional policing aspect that appears to have dwindled in The Gambia is the Beat Patrol. Although we had learned about beat patrols and the police notebook, their practical implementation was rare. It seems that beat patrols were conducted only when crime rates surged and ceased when crime rates declined. This pattern was evident in operations like Operation Bulldozer, Operation No Compromise, Anti-Crime, and Operation Zero Crime.

For many police officers, work primarily involves reporting to duty and awaiting the reporting of crimes. If crime rates are low at a police station, some officers may complain of having no work.

Gallery of Photos

My parents and I

With my older cousin Pa Kujabi

With my sister Veronic, and my cousin Tubabo

On the first day at the training school, just after the baptism

Evenings at the Police Training School

Group photo during Cadet Officer Training at PTS

A group photo with IGP Sonko a day before we left for Ghana

The Ghana Chronicles

Group photo with DSP Pokoo Aikins the College Directing Staff

Cadet Officers in gentlemanly fashion during social evenings at the college

President John Mahama addressing the officers at the graduation

Cadet Officers Omar D Bah, myself and Muhammed Lamin Sonko

M L Sonko and I at the inauguration of the Police Lines in Banjul

You ng Cadet Officer David Kujabi

With Omar D Bah posed in front of the Mounted Squadron

My days as Police PRO

My days as Police PRO

Me, leading the Christian prayers during the inauguration of the Banjulinnding Police Station in 2015

L – R CP Lala Camara, ASP Abdou Bojang, myself, CP Ebrima Bah, …… Kuyateh, CSP Yaya Touray, CP Ceesay, DIG Edu Sambou, and CP Kebba Bojang during the inauguration of the Police Lines

Pictures from my peacekeeping in Darfur, Sudan

With officers of the Indonesian Formed Police Unit during patrols in Elfasher

Interviewing IDP leaders to gather stories for UNAMID Police Chronicle

A serious and Cheery looking David

The Birth of **POLISO** Magazine

My initial months as a police officer were marked by the challenges of adapting to a significantly reduced salary compared to my previous job. Nevertheless, I was passionate about my new role and its daily trials, immersing myself in it and diligently learning from my colleagues and various policing literature. During this period, I couldn't help but notice a substantial communication gap between the police force and the public. While the police diligently uphold law and order and protect lives and property, the public did not recognise and appreciate their efforts.

During these reflections, the idea of bridging this gap through creating a police magazine began to take shape. I shared this vision with my colleagues, Abdou Bojang and Lamin Njie, and they were quick to embrace the concept as an effective means of connecting with the public. Together, we composed a proposal outlining our vision for a police magazine and submitted it to Commissioner Abdoulie Sanyang, who was responsible for reviewing and approving such initiatives.

However, for reasons beyond our comprehension, our proposal seemed to languish in bureaucratic limbo, taking what felt like an eternity to reach Commissioner Sanyang's desk. Along its convoluted journey through the chain of command, some individuals questioned our aspirations or underestimated our commitment to this endeavour.

After what felt like an interminable wait, I finally approached Commissioner Sanyang personally to inquire if he had received our proposal regarding the magazine. To my surprise, he had not seen it, and I promptly provided him with a copy. As he perused our proposal, he became visibly excited and offered his support on the condition that we could guarantee the production and sustainability of the magazine. Without hesitation, I confidently assured him that we could meet this commitment.

True to his word, Commissioner Sanyang secured approval from Inspector General of Police Yankuba Sonko for our undertaking. IGP Sonko permitted us and extended his unwavering support to the POLISO team throughout his tenure. I hold IGP Sonko in the highest regard and attribute my career's foundation to his guidance and encouragement.

In May 2011, I was tasked with producing the inaugural edition of the Gambia Police Force Magazine, POLISO. Despite limited resources, our unwavering commitment, supported by the trust and backing of IGP Sonko and Commissioner Abdoulie Sonko, served as our driving force.

During this phase, Lamin Njie was on cadet rotation in Soma, while Abdou Bojang was stationed in Bansang. Despite the geographical distance, these dedicated colleagues actively contributed to our publication's success. On my end, I functioned as a one-person team on the ground, operating without a designated office space. Ansumana Kinteh (then Superintendent of Police) was the Commanding Officer in the Human Resource Office. Kinteh was the youngest senior police officer who worked tirelessly to ensure the magazine's success. Kinteh hosted me in his office and facilitated for me to get a laptop to use to start the magazine. Luckily, the Independent Electoral Commission (IEC) had recently donated GPF a few laptops from the ones they used to conduct voter registration. I was handed a fairly used one. In his office, I had no table; all I had was a chair, and I used my lap as a table. Kinteh, however, made me very welcome and comfortable in his office, and together, we worked to publish a maiden edition of a police magazine by July 22 2011.

Another person who was quite helpful in ensuring the publication of the police magazine was Malick Mboob, a banker who was once a journalist. He was hired as a consultant to help us through the journey. For my part, I began by compiling stories and in parallel, I initiated correspondence by writing letters to all police commissioners, seeking their input and support for our magazine. We also approached various institutions, companies, and organisations, soliciting their interest in advertising in our maiden police magazine.

During follow-up calls to these entities, it became apparent that many found the notion of the police producing a magazine incredulous. Some did not hide their scepticism about the police's capability to undertake such a venture. Rather than dampen our spirits, their cynicism served as fuel, strengthening our resolve to see our magazine come to fruition. It is worth noting that this scepticism was not confined to external stakeholders; even within the police ranks, there was significant doubt.

Among the few senior police officers who responded to our request for input were Commissioner Mamour Jobe, the Commandant of the Police Training School; Commissioner Aziz Y Bojang of the Peacekeeping Centre; and Commissioner Aminata L Ndour of the West Coast Region. While several other commissioners offered suggestions, they did not significantly contribute to our cause. Various magazine name suggestions were put forth, including *"Samakatt," "Crime Stoppers,"* and others, which we did not find particularly appealing.

In search of a local and impactful name, we proposed "POLISO." After careful consideration, my colleagues unanimously agreed that it encapsulated the essence of our magazine perfectly, and thus, the name was established.

As we compiled stories and secured support from advertisers, I vividly recall one incident that left a lasting impression. It was a mix of embarrassment and humility. I was working on a story detailing the efforts of Chief Superintendent Landing Bojang, the Operations Commander of Serrekunda, in combatting crime in the area. I had already interviewed him but needed photographs of the patrol team. Accordingly, I sought permission from Officer Commanding (OC) Samba Jawo to join the afternoon patrol team in Serrekunda. A vehicle was en route to Serrekunda, which I intended to join, but I knew I did not have sufficient funds to cover my return fare home once my task was completed.

Upon contacting OC Jawo and informing him of my visit, I specifically requested that Commander Bojang be notified of my need for transportation. I hoped that he would provide transport for my return journey. I travelled to Serrekunda and participated in a patrol that combed through crime-prone areas like Shanghai and Hannover. The cover photo of our first magazine edition was captured while officers were searching for a group of boys in the Hannover area.

Upon the patrol's conclusion, I reported to Commander Bojang, anticipating his assistance with transport back home. However, he expressed his gratitude and bid me farewell without making transportation arrangements. I then realised that his interpretation of OC Jawo's request to provide transport was limited to allowing me to join the patrol team. I had only five Dalasis in my pocket, two short of the seven Dalasis required for the fare to Lamin.

With embarrassment, I made my way to the car park, uncertain of my next steps. It was a little after 4 PM, and the park bustled with commuters eager to return home. I approached some drivers and asked if they would accept five Dalasis for the fare. However, the first two drivers I approached firmly stated that the fare was seven Dalasis. My embarrassment heightened, and I began to perspire, still clad in my white police uniform.

Standing there, uncertain and distressed, I suddenly felt a gentle touch on my hand. I turned to see a young apprentice, no older than fourteen, who discreetly placed two Dalasi coins into my palm and urged me to board the vehicle. I complied and found a seat in a corner; my face flushed with embarrassment throughout the journey back to Lamin.

We completed the magazine by dint of hard work, sacrifice, and great teamwork. On July 22 2011, the first edition of POLISO magazine was published. The day I held a printed copy of the magazine, I cried, reflecting on challenges, scepticism, and outright prediction of failure in our venture.

The first edition of POLISO received an overwhelmingly positive response and was met with immense pride and joy by the police force personnel. Our achievement was a collective triumph, and we wasted no time commencing work on the second edition, slated for publication in December.

Eager to outdo AHOOAH, the magazine produced by the Gambia Armed Forces, we aspired to feature an exclusive interview with President Yahya Jammeh in the upcoming edition. To pursue this, we submitted a letter to the Office of the President, requesting an audience for the interview. In response, we were asked to present our intended questions.

Commissioner Abdoulie instructed us to draft our questions and share them for review. However, one question we included led to shelving our interview idea. We had inquired whether the president believed that the frequent changes in the Inspector General of Police (IGP) position hindered the force's growth, as each new appointment disrupted the continuity of vision and plans. While we believed the question was legitimate, we were informed that we could not pose it to the president and commander-in-chief. In hindsight, I understand the command's decision, which likely preserved the magazine's existence. At that time, we were too inexperienced to grasp the intricacies of politics and the dynamics within the corridors of power.

From when Yahya Jammeh assumed power in July 1994 until 2011, there were twelve different IGPs, some serving for less than a year. Notable among these appointments was Pa Sallah Jagne, a former IGP who had served under President Jawara and was removed in 1994 after the coup. Another surprising appointment was Rex King, a retired Fire Officer from June 1999 to June 2000. Ousman Sonko, a military captain, was appointed IGP in April 2004 and served until September 2007. Musa Mboob, previously the Director General of the Immigration Department, was redeployed as IGP from April 2007 to June 2008. None of these appointees were career policemen, except Musa Mboob, who had trained in the Gendarmerie, a military force with law enforcement powers. Benedict Jammeh, an Assistant Superintendent of Police (ASP), was appointed IGP but served briefly before being replaced. Benn Wilson, a retired military officer, was appointed Commissioner of Police and later served as IGP.

These appointments, often involving non-police personnel, were met with disapproval within the police force ranks. Officers were preoccupied with the fear of losing their jobs instead of concentrating on their professional duties. Pleasing the whims of the presidency became a priority for most IGPs, leading to a challenging balance between what was right and what was desired by the commander-in-chief. It was a running joke among us that Yahya Jammeh never visited the police headquarters nor attended any police function despite numerous invitations. This further fuelled the perception that he was not particularly supportive of the police force, unlike his interactions with the army.

Politics and Policing: A Delicate Balance

The Gambia Police Force (GPF) is our nation's bedrock of law and order. Entrusted with the authority to maintain order, prevent crime, enforce laws, and prosecute offenders, the GPF ensures that the government retains its stability and respectability within society, as outlined in Chapter XII (12) of The Gambia's constitution.

In theory, the role of the police is inclusive, and the law applies to all. Regrettably, political influence has sometimes hindered the full realisation of this principle. Politics, often characterised as the art of wielding authority over the government and public affairs, significantly impacts the appointments of key positions within the criminal justice system, including the Inspector General of Police (IGP), judges, and Directors General of agencies like Immigration and Prisons.

The ramifications of political influence extend far and wide, potentially resulting in the promotion of personal interests within government, dominance in government leadership, control over resources, and occupation of key governmental positions. Consequently, there exists the risk of the police force acting in a manner that favours particular individuals or groups over the equitable enforcement of the law.

Preserving the independence of the police force from political pressures is paramount. This independence ensures that justice prevails and the rule of law is upheld. The GPF must operate autonomously to maintain its credibility and public trust, upholding a stable and respected society.

Local government officials, such as mayors, are elected representatives whose priorities may naturally align with the interests of those who elected them. On the other hand, service chiefs are typically appointed by the highest political authority. Such appointments can lead to influences that resonate deeply within the police force.

A police force is entrusted with maintaining order and preventing crime within the governance framework. Yet, when political affiliations start influencing the selective enforcement of laws, targeting political adversaries or perceived "threatening" groups, it can result in widespread corruption and the abuse of power. Unfortunately, this shadow of corruption has dominated police forces throughout history.

The story of policing in The Gambia is intricately interwoven with the nation's political evolution. Its origins trace back to 1855, when it was established by Her Majesty's government, initially known as the River Police. Their duties encompassed maintaining law and order, suppressing rebellions, and combating smuggling on land and sea. However, their primary allegiance lay with the colonial authorities.

Over time, the force transformed, with the pivotal year of 1888 marking its rebranding as the Gambia Police Force (GPF), adapting to serve the needs of the colonial administration, which included protecting the governor and other officials.

In 1958, the Field Force emerged as a police paramilitary unit entrusted with external security. Upon The Gambia's independence in 1965, the GPF continued to prioritise maintaining law and order, with the head of the force appointed by the head of state. This status quo persisted during the three-decade rule of the People Progressive Party (PPP), with seven IGPs appointed by the head of state during that era.

A pivotal shift occurred following the failed coup attempt in 1981. The Field Force was disbanded, giving rise to the Gambia National Army and Gambia National Gendarmerie. The latter held dual military and police powers, significantly transforming the nation's security landscape.

Ultimately, the narrative of policing in The Gambia remains a captivating and intricate tale closely entwined with the country's political trajectory over the years.

In July 1994, a military coup replaced the PPP regime with the Armed Forces Ruling Provisional Ruling Council (AFPRC), which was later transformed into the Alliance for Patriotic Reorientation and Construction (APRC) for two years. During its 22-year rule, the GPF witnessed the appointment of 12 IGPs, some serving terms as brief as six months. This serves as an illustration of the substantial influence that the government exerted over police leadership. Officers' hiring, dismissal, and promotion often depended on their loyalty to the political leadership.

The intricate relationship between politics and policing has been the subject of extensive research, revealing that political influence over the police can yield adverse consequences. When politicians wield control over police appointments and operations, they may exploit their authority to advance personal political agendas, including manipulating the police force to selectively enforce laws against political adversaries and rewarding political allies with preferential treatment. This often culminates in corruption and abuse of power, as police officers may feel compelled to align with the interests of their political superiors.

Security sector reform must be prioritised to counteract this issue, focusing on mitigating political influence within the police force. This can be achieved by implementing democratic policing and community policing models that operate independently from political patronage systems. Police leadership must actively safeguard the operational autonomy of the police force, shielding it from political interference but adhering to civilian oversight. This can be accomplished through civil service protection for police heads and establishing service contracts that hold them accountable for their department's actions rather than subjecting them to the whims of political authorities.

In conclusion, the intersection of politics and the police is a critical concern that impacts the legitimacy and efficacy of the police force within society. Political interference in policing can erode public trust and confidence in law enforcement, ultimately undermining the rule of law. The security sector reform process must prioritise the independence and integrity of the police force in carrying out their duties without political interference, coupled with robust civilian oversight to ensure accountability of the force.

Officers' Course in Ghana: A Transformative Journey

In November 2011, a pivotal opportunity emerged when IGP Sonko returned from an IGPs conference with groundbreaking news: he had secured ten coveted slots for cadet officers to embark on a transformative six-month Cadet Officers Course at the prestigious Ghana Police College. I was among the fortunate few, and with no time to spare, we were swiftly instructed to prepare for the journey, as the course was already in progress.

Nestled in Tesano, Accra, the Ghana Police College (GPC) was established in 1959 as an esteemed Higher Educational Institution of the Ghana Police Service. Its mission was to deliver top-tier professional and practical training, enhancing the command, staff, operational, and managerial capabilities of senior police officers.

Our cohort was aptly named Course 44, signifying that we were the 44th group of officers to undergo training since the college's inception. Here, I truly grasped the essence of policing—a more profound understanding, an enriched appreciation, and a newfound love for this vocation. This experience was equally illuminating in highlighting the areas where The Gambia Police Force needed development, emphasising the significance of elevating the value and respect accorded to service personnel. Policing was a highly esteemed profession, underscored by competitive entry requirements and enticing remuneration packages.

Tesano was not just home to the Police College; it resembled a veritable police village, housing diverse units such as the Police Training School, the Police Band, the Criminal Investigations Academy, the Armoured Car Squadron, the Police Band (again), the Formed Police Unit, and quarters for both senior officers and non-commissioned officers (NCOs). Markets, bars, restaurants, and mess facilities abound. Our makeshift training school in The Gambia paled compared to these extensive facilities.

Our officer training transcended practical policing, command, and leadership—it was an initiation into the esteemed officer cadre of the police services. Within the service culture, two primary categories existed: NCOs and the Officer Corps. Entry into the Officer Corps was not simply a matter of seniority but rather a rigorous process that groomed individuals for their officer roles. It was akin to joining an exclusive society, necessitating a distinct mindset. Officers were tasked with leadership and managerial roles, demanding the selection of the finest and most capable personnel.

In Ghana, entry into the Officer Corps mandated passage through the Police College. It was subject to NCOs at the rank of Chief Inspector successfully sitting and passing an entrance examination. Additionally, Police Officers recruited as professionals, such as doctors, nurses, engineers, etc., were eligible for the college.

The Gambian scenario, however, starkly contrasted with this model, contributing to many of the security service problems witnessed during the 22-year rule of President Jammeh. Most security services lacked a coherent promotion policy, with service chiefs wielding arbitrary authority over promotions. These promotions often bypassed merit-based criteria, relying instead on personal relationships or executive influence. Some individuals ascended through multiple ranks in short timeframes. I distinctly recall a Minister of Interior recommending a corporal for promotion to sergeant due to his impressive command presence and marching skills during a ceremonial quarter guard.

The Ghana experience proved both enlightening and rigorous. It forged officers out of us and moulded us into refined gentlemen. Alongside our Gambian contingent were ten officers from the Liberia Police Service, and strict adherence to rules was paramount. We were confined to barracks except for monthly exeat Saturdays, granting us limited freedom from 10:00 am to 5:00 pm. A stringent dress code was enforced, with violations subject to penalties. Our drill attire comprised neatly pressed long brown khaki trousers, marching shirts, and pristine black combat boots. We sported navy blue shirts and trousers with black loafers in the classroom. We wore long black trousers, a white long-sleeved shirt, and a black tie for evening mess. Officer etiquette and conduct standards became second nature.

Amidst our adherence to these standards, we humorously contemplated the challenges of maintaining such exacting criteria back home in The Gambia. The most glaring obstacle was our meagre salaries, which fell short of supporting the lifestyle expected of an officer. While the Ghana Police Service provided some educational resources, others were to be procured independently, a financial burden we often struggled with. To cope, we resorted to photocopying sections of required books. Additionally, we learned that our Ghanaian peers preferred bottled water over tap water. To economise, we discreetly refilled empty bottles with tap water while pretending to consume bottled water exclusively.

Despite these trials, we Gambians forged a formidable esprit de corps throughout the training. We wholeheartedly supported and encouraged one another. During leisure, we often congregated to brew and share *ataya*—a ritual that attracted the curious interest of fellow trainees who believed it enhanced one's virility, adding a peculiar twist to our camaraderie.

The course was divided into two semesters, each culminating in an examination. During the initial semester, I was dedicated, punctual, and studious, spending hours in the library. However, by the second semester, my adventurous side emerged. I formed a close friendship with Yancy Blama, a Liberian Police Officer who mirrored my penchant for exploration. We frequented the Officers' mess, sampled Ghanaian beer, and expanded our social circles beyond our coursemates. Soon, we began venturing out beyond the confines of our barracks at night to explore Kokomlemle, Abeka, and Kaneshie.

My roommate, Muhammed Lamin Sonko, often chastised my perceived unruly behaviour. He conscientiously adhered to every college rule and rarely left the campus, dedicating his evenings to watching TV in the anteroom. He could have easily been awarded the title of the most compliant officer, except for one lapse just before our course's conclusion when he broke a rule and was caught.

To facilitate our stipend distribution, we opened a collective bank account, with Sonko entrusted to manage the funds. However, during our final month before graduation, our stipends arrived, and due to my financial strain, I urged Sonko to collect the money on our behalf. On a Saturday, after our physical training session, I convinced Sonko to withdraw the funds, assuring him that his absence for a few hours would go unnoticed. Unfortunately, our timing coincided with a surprise roll call summoned by Deputy Commissioner of Police Yaagy Akuriba, the Commandant of the College. Several officers, including Sonko, were absent. The Commandant incensed and mandated a daily punishment: during lunch hours, the defaulters were required to change into their drill outfits, collect rifles from the armoury, and briskly march around the parade ground under the blazing sun. As I prepared to head to the mess for lunch each day, I witnessed Sonko donning his drill attire, enduring the punishing heat. At first, I teased him, highlighting the irony of his predicament as a grown man with two wives representing The Gambia, yet facing punishment for flouting rules. However, as the days passed, I ceased my jests, recognising the severity of his situation.

Unfortunately, the six-month intensive training program stretched to nine months due to unforeseen circumstances. We completed the training within six months and were poised for graduation. However, this was postponed due to the illness of then-President John Atta Mills. Although not a legal requirement, it was customary for the president to commission officers into the Ghana Police Service. Consequently, we patiently waited three more months as President Mills battled his illness. Regrettably, he succumbed, and on 24 July 2012, President John Atta Mills passed away. Subsequently, Vice President John Mahama assumed office, and on 1 August 2012, we finally graduated in a vibrant and colourful ceremony, with Foday Fofana winning the Best Foreign Officer Award. With newfound knowledge, enthusiasm, and preparedness, we returned to The Gambia on 4 August as well-trained officers, ready to serve our nation with dedication and commitment.

My Journey as the Police PRO

We, the Commissioned Officers appointed by the President of Ghana, returned to our homeland, still bearing the title of Cadet Officers until 2013. During this transformative year, I was entrusted with a surprise appointment as the Public Relations Officer (PRO) of The Gambia Police Force. Although my passion for writing and past success with the POLISO project was well-known, I lacked formal journalism or public relations training. My sole exposure to Public Relations was a single lecture during our officer's course in Ghana. To this day, I remain uncertain who proposed my appointment, but I owe a debt of gratitude to that individual as it set the course for much of my career. From the outset, I was determined to give my best and honour the trust bestowed upon me.

However, my journey as a PRO was not without its share of challenges. I stepped into the role when it was vacant, lacking mentorship or formal training. The previous PRO, Yorro Mballow, had been reassigned before our return from Ghana. Approximately a week after my appointment, Yorro formally handed over the office to me and provided an overview of my responsibilities. At that time, this seemed adequate, but it was fraught with challenges in hindsight. No clearly defined Terms of Reference (TOR) existed for the Office of the PRO or the PRO position, nor were there Key Performance Management Indicators (KPIs). All I was told was that I was the voice of the Gambia Police Force, tasked with conducting press briefings, addressing media inquiries, and participating in traffic radio talk shows. Yet, my role extended beyond being a mere spokesperson; it encompassed projecting and promoting a positive image of the force. Despite the absence of formal guidance, I persevered, learning on the job, and over time, I made significant strides in enhancing the relationship between the police and the public.

However, the true baptism of fire came swiftly. While I cannot recall the precise day of my appointment, as it was conveyed verbally rather than through a formal letter, I vividly remember the day former PRO Mballow officially passed the torch to me. Among the items transferred to me was a mobile SIM card with the official phone number for the Police PRO: 9968885. I recall that date was August 27, 2012, not because of the handover but due to the momentous events that transpired later that day.

After concluding my workday, I replaced my personal SIM card with the official PRO's SIM card, as I had no dedicated phone. Shortly after that, the phone rang an international call. Filled with trepidation, I answered in what I hoped was an appropriately official tone. On the other end of the line was a lady who identified herself as a reporter from Radio France International (RFI). She sought information about the execution of nine death row inmates at the Mile Two Central Prisons the previous night, which had occurred on Sunday, August 26, 2012.

Initially, I was clueless about the matter and conveyed as much to her. At that moment, the daunting and perilous nature of my role as Police PRO truly hit me. I realised I would be tasked with addressing many sensitive national security issues. I quickly learned what to say, what not to say, whom to communicate with, and how to convey information.

The following week, The Gambia was rocked by unusual events: three murder cases transpired in a single night. These included the gruesome murder of a lady by her sister-in-law in Brusubi, a young man killed in London Corner, and the death of a 15-year-old male burglar. My responsibility was to report these incidents to the media. Despite my inexperience with television and radio appearances, the entire Gambian media turned to me for information.

Despite my initial lack of training, I evolved into a seasoned communications expert, extending my expertise beyond security. As the PRO for the Gambia Police Force, I effectively bridged the gap between the police and the public. I introduced numerous radio programs and, for the first time, spearheaded a live television talk show called the "Community Policing Hour." The rapport with the media improved, and information regarding crime and policing became more accessible.

Entering the world of public relations as a novice devoid of formal training, I successfully met the demands of my role as the Police PRO.

My tenure saw significant enhancements in the relationship between the police and the public. I introduced several radio programs, including the pioneering "Community Policing Hour" on television. The improved relationship with the media ensured that information related to crime and policing was readily disseminated. This positive engagement with the public inspired many young people, particularly university and college graduates, to consider joining the police force. I navigated rewarding and challenging moments in this role, with numerous stories and experiences, some of which remain bound by the oath of secrecy.

During my officer's course at the Ghana Police College, a lecturer made a statement that resonated with me throughout my tenure as a public relations officer in the security sector: "There is a lot of news in the bosom of the police." While this statement holds great appeal for journalists, it poses challenges for communications and public relations practitioners tasked with promoting the positive image of a security institution. Not all news is marketable, and the intricacies of security provision, particularly in relation to fundamental human rights, often generate a mix of good and bad news. More often than not, negative news garners greater public interest, creating situations PR professionals would rather avoid. Another challenge lies in navigating confidential information with national security implications, highlighting the delicate balance between the right to access information and safeguarding national security.

Communications and PR in the security sector demand tact, caution, and a nuanced understanding of what information to share, when to share it, and how to convey it. Effective communication necessitates strong listening skills, patience, tolerance, and adaptability. In some instances, written communication proves more prudent than verbal discourse, allowing control over the narrative and avoiding unwelcome questions. Additionally, wit, charm, and the ability to build rapport are indispensable skills that can positively influence communication in the security sector.

One of the significant challenges I faced was the absence of friends within the media fraternity, as each journalist sought an exclusive scoop. It was imperative never to let my guard down. Furthermore, the role of a PR professional representing the Gambia Police Force meant assuming the mantle of the force's image, both professionally and personally. Every word and action was scrutinised not as David Kujabi but as the Police PRO.

Despite the myriad challenges, I embraced the job with enthusiasm. One of the most exhilarating aspects of my role was the opportunity to network and establish relationships with individuals from diverse backgrounds. Over the years, I discovered that my role not only allowed me to promote and enhance the organisation's image but also empowered me to instil confidence and hope in my audience. It facilitated mutual understanding and trust, for which people were profoundly grateful, a deeply satisfying aspect of my work. In numerous instances involving unpleasant issues typical of the security sector, I endeavoured to allay fears, restore hope, instil confidence, and assure justice. The sense of satisfaction derived from the public's reassurance, coupled with the enhancement of my institution's reputation and the cultivation of public trust, brought me immense joy.

Arresting a Military Officer: A Risky Act of Duty

During my tenure as a police officer, I experienced a pivotal moment when I had to make a crucial arrest. In early 2015, while commuting from work to Lamin, I encountered a situation that demanded immediate action. Traffic had reached a standstill near the Latrikunda market, particularly on the stretch leading to Tabokoto.

As I navigated the congested road, I was drawn to a military truck travelling in the same direction but on the opposing lane. Not only was this a clear violation of traffic rules, but it also disrupted the flow of vehicles on that side of the road. Regrettably, such occurrences were not uncommon among security personnel when on official missions.

The driver's behaviour was reckless, disregarding proper lane usage. On the other side of the road, I observed a female pedestrian patiently waiting to cross safely. When an opportunity arose, she stepped onto the road just as the military truck, travelling from an unexpected direction, collided with her, causing her to fall heavily in the middle of the thoroughfare.

To my astonishment, the military driver continued without stopping to aid the injured woman, callously leaving her sprawled on the road. A compassionate taxi driver intervened, assisted by pedestrians in lifting the injured woman into his vehicle, and rushed her towards the Faji Kunda Health Centre.

Infuriated by the soldier's actions, I decided to take matters into my own hands. Near the Faji Kunda clinic, I manoeuvred my vehicle onto the opposite lane, blocking traffic and compelling the military truck to a halt. Confronting the driver, I inquired whether he was aware of his actions. His response indicated that he was on an urgent mission to Kanilai, tasked with delivering a generator for the Roots Homecoming Festival hosted by the president.

Undeterred, I insisted he follow me to the health centre to assess the victim's condition. Despite pleas from his fellow soldiers, I maintained my position, and he complied. Throughout the journey to the health centre, I contacted Commissioner of Traffic Fadia Jarjou, urging her to dispatch traffic officers to the scene.

At the health centre, a medical examination confirmed the victim's unconscious state, necessitating her referral to Banjul for further treatment.

The significance of this incident transcended a mere traffic accident. It was about arresting a military officer at a time when the military held considerable power and often acted with impunity. It was a period marked by frequent flouting of traffic regulations by military personnel and instances of police officers being assaulted while trying to execute their duties.

As the minutes passed with no sign of traffic officers, a senior military official arrived, urging me to release the driver to prevent further delays in his mission. The situation grew increasingly tense, and I began to worry about potential repercussions. Despite my concerns, the gathering crowd of civilians reinforced my conviction to do what was right, even if it meant risking my job.

In this moment of uncertainty, I reached out to Inspector General of Police Benn Wilson, who emphatically instructed me to stand my ground. After what felt like an eternity, the awaited traffic officers finally arrived. I entrusted them with the case and departed, a mix of satisfaction for doing what was right and anxiety about the potential consequences of my actions.

Peacekeeping in Darfur

Nestled in the western expanse of Sudan, the sprawling region of Darfur, spanning 510,888 square kilometres, stands as one of Sudan's states. It is divided into five administrative regions: North, South, East, West, and Central, each under the leadership of a locally termed "Wali" or governor. Before 2012, it comprised only the North, South, and Central regions. Islam is the predominant religion, and as of 2010, Darfur's population was estimated at approximately 7.5 million, representing over 100 distinct tribes. However, these tribes were broadly categorised into sedentary African farmers and nomadic Arab tribes. Tensions among these groups had simmered for years, but Darfur erupted into a cauldron of conflict in the late 1980s, with death and displacement persisting until 2015.

The intensification of the conflict is often traced back to a fateful event on February 26, 2003, when a group known as the Darfur Liberation Front (DLF) launched an attack on a military garrison in the town of Golo. While violence had simmered for years, this incident catalysed a major war that unleashed devastating consequences upon the region.

In response to the deteriorating situation, the African Union Mission in Sudan (AMIS) emerged in 2004 as a peacekeeping operation. Comprising military and civilian personnel from various African nations, AMIS aimed to monitor ceasefires, facilitate peace agreements, and ensure security for humanitarian assistance. In 2005, the Gambia Police Force (GPF) joined this mission, dispatching a contingent of 35 officers led by Superintendent Saihou Njie. This marked the beginning of GPF's invaluable contribution to the Darfur peace process, following similar efforts in Liberia, Kosovo, and Timor-Leste, also known as East Timor.

Despite noble intentions, AMIS grappled with numerous challenges, including limited resources, insufficient troop strength, and difficulties enforcing peace agreements. The mission struggled to contain the escalating violence, prompting escalating calls for a more robust international intervention.

The United Nations and the African Union collaborated to establish the African Union-United Nations Hybrid Operation in Darfur (UNAMID) to address these challenges. United Nations Security Council Resolution 1769, adopted on July 31, 2007, formalised the creation of UNAMID. This joint mission, officially commencing on December 31, 2007, was endowed with a comprehensive mandate: protecting civilians, facilitating humanitarian aid, mediating between conflicting parties, monitoring agreement implementations, and promoting human rights in Darfur.

Participating in a peacekeeping mission held an immense allure for many police officers, offering not only international experience but also substantial income. The prospect of higher wages had significant appeal, particularly given the modest salaries of police officers, making it challenging to secure personal assets like homes. A single year of peacekeeping could provide the financial stability needed to purchase land and build a modest residence.

In 2015, I was fortunate to be deployed as a Police Advisor to Darfur after a rigorous and lengthy selection process. The allure of peacekeeping had captivated my fellow cadet officers and me since our training days. Thus, when we learned that the United Nations Selection Assistance and Assessment Team (SAAT) would conduct an assessment in The Gambia, we eagerly submitted our names for consideration. Although I passed the exam, deployment occurred over a year after the SAAT. SAAT exam results were valid for two years, and any successful candidate not deployed within that period forfeited eligibility. The anxious wait for news of deployment was palpable.

My peacekeeping experience proved transformative in many ways, particularly in shaping my perceptions of conflict, war, and peace. United Nations peacekeeping operations typically consist of three components: civilian, military, and police. UNAMID's success hinged on the collaboration of these three facets. The civilian component focused on political processes, humanitarian assistance, human rights protection, and upholding the rule of law. The military component provided security, patrolled the region, safeguarded civilians, and facilitated aid delivery. In 2015, UNAMID's Police mandate encompassed supporting the physical protection of civilians, facilitating humanitarian assistance, and creating a protective environment through government police capacity development and community-oriented policing activities. The synergy of these components aimed to comprehensively address the multifaceted challenges in the region, promoting sustainable peace and development.

After completing our Initial Induction Training, two fellow Gambian Police Officers, Abdoulie Jallow, Mariama Jahateh, and I, were deployed to the Mukjar Team Site in Central Darfur. I served as a patrol officer for three months before being reassigned to the Public Information Office at the headquarters in Elfasher. As patrol officers, we conducted confidence-building patrols around Internally Displaced Persons (IDP) camps. These patrols involved engaging with IDPs, seeking their input on the security situation in their area, conditions at the IDP camps, and their general welfare. We also organised classes for IDP children, teaching them the English language. Furthermore, we liaised with officers of the Sudan Police Force to share best practices and promote a community policing approach in their operations.

While these efforts may sound commendable, the reality posed challenges. In certain IDP camps, people hesitated to interact with peacekeepers, often walking away when a patrol convoy approached. Routine interactions had become monotonous and unproductive. Our inquiries primarily focused on gathering information for our reports, covering aspects such as the visited location, the names and backgrounds of individuals interacted with, their ages, tribes, and any security incidents they wished to report.

Beyond the standard feedback collected for reporting purposes, I yearned for deeper insight into the experiences and perceptions of IDPs, particularly regarding the conflict and peacekeeping efforts. To achieve this, I collaborated with a local United Nations Department of Safety and Security (UNDSS) officer named Alhardy to interview IDPs. I delved into topics such as their initial encounters with the war and its impact on their lives, their sentiments upon the arrival of peacekeepers, and their current perspectives on the peacekeeping endeavour. These interviews, conducted in October 2015, revealed compelling personal narratives of war and frustration. While expressing gratitude for the peacekeeping efforts, interviewees also voiced their discontent with the slow pace of peace and the enduring consequences of the conflict. Two years later, this frustration persisted. In an interview conducted during my tenure as Public Information Officer to gauge IDPs' opinions on the downsizing of UNAMID, one respondent poignantly expressed disappointment, stating, "Over ten years ago, UNAMID found me in an IDP camp, and now they are preparing to leave while I am still in an IDP camp."

My role at the Public Information Office (PIO), where I eventually became the Head of PIO, allowed me to play a pivotal role in enhancing the image of the UNAMID Police Component. One of our primary responsibilities was producing a weekly newsletter spotlighting the accomplishments of UNAMID Police across all Darfur regions. This undertaking gave me invaluable insights into the mission's positive interventions, encompassing Quick Intervention Projects (QIPS), livelihood activities, and individual police contributions. In sum, UNAMID reduced armed conflicts, facilitated access to previously inaccessible areas, enhanced support for mediation between the Government of Sudan and armed movements, and reinforced traditional community-based mechanisms through community policing in IDP camps.

Police Advisors in peacekeeping missions do not receive a salary but are provided with a Mission Subsistence Allowance (MSA). Throughout our tenure, this allowance amounted to USD 136, accumulating and paid at the end of each month. This DSA, approximately USD 4000 per month, was intended to cover various expenses, including lodging, meals, and other necessities.

However, GPF policy mandated that peacekeeping personnel contribute 10% of their DSA to the police force to support staff welfare. Notable projects funded by these contributions included uniform purchases and construction or renovation of police stations, such as Bakoteh, Banjulinding, Jarra Bureng, Bakadaji, and Ndugu Kebbeh Police Stations.

Beyond individual 10% contributions, contingents took additional initiatives to enhance GPF welfare. Our contingent, led by now-retired Commissioner Malamin Ceesay, undertook a unique project to construct a standard cafeteria at the Police Training School using our monthly contributions.

When our contingent committed to the cafeteria project, I was tasked with finding a suitable design. I collaborated with Inspector Kebba Jobe, an architect with the GPF engineering unit, who created an exceptional design. The proposed plan met with the contingent's approval and, after GPF command review, received construction authorisation. According to the agreement, we covered material costs while the GPF Engineering Unit handled construction.

The project commenced in early 2017, making significant progress. The building had been roofed by our departure in October of the same year. Regrettably, work halted upon our return. Despite updates on the funds sent for the project, a substantial balance remained to continue construction. Sadly, there was no further communication or explanation regarding the remaining funds. The fate of these funds mirrored the need for more accountability for Individual Police Officers' contributions to peacekeeping missions.

The building remained unfinished until 2023, when it was eventually completed as part of the Police Training School's renovation efforts, led by the German Police Support Team (GPST). Surprisingly, during the inauguration in March 2023, there was no acknowledgement of our contingent's significant contribution to the cafeteria's construction.

The Psychology of Service Personnel

In 2018, I was honoured to receive a Rotary Peace Scholarship, which allowed me to pursue a master's degree in Peace Conflict and Development at the University of Bradford in the United Kingdom. My motivation for choosing this path was deeply rooted in my experiences during the Darfur conflict and my aspiration to comprehend the intricate dynamics of conflicts to make a meaningful contribution to peace.

During my academic journey in May 2019, I embarked on a study tour in Northern Ireland, where a remarkable encounter reshaped my perspective on military and police service mentalities. Our group had the privilege of meeting an ex-British soldier who had served during the tumultuous period known as 'The Troubles' (1968-1998). These were years marked by violent conflict between Protestant Unionists (loyalists) and Roman Catholic Nationalists (republicans), with the Irish Republican Army (IRA) arising from the latter group.

The former soldier's candid discussion highlighted the psychological transformation during military and service training. He conveyed how the training instils a sense of belonging to a brotherhood, fostering unwavering loyalty to one's country and the belief that one's nation is always on the right side of any conflict. Interestingly, he mentioned that soldiers often do not harbour personal animosity toward their perceived adversaries but are willing to engage in violence for political reasons.

This revelation prompted me to ponder the similar mentality among police officers, who sometimes disperse demonstrators forcefully even when the causes are just. The training processes for military and police personnel appear to cultivate an 'Us versus Them' mindset. My initiation into the police force involved instructors who aimed to erase our civilian identities and mould us into security service personnel akin to soldiers.

While reflecting on my training experiences in The Gambia and Ghana, I realised that programs designed to produce law enforcement officers and protectors of life and property may inadvertently yield individuals who do not fully grasp the nuances of civic-centred security values. A research paper by Hills succinctly describes African police forces as generally "brutal, corrupt, and badly paid," a characterisation I initially hesitated to accept but felt compelled to scrutinise objectively.

This revelation illuminated the complex psyche of security personnel, explaining their seemingly callous actions, such as dispersing demonstrators even in cases where the demands are valid and beneficial to the police themselves. The training, I realised, perpetuates an 'Us versus Them' mentality, eroding the empathetic connection between law enforcers and civilians. As a fledgling police officer, I distinctly remember being told that our civilian identity would be effaced, replaced by the demeanour and mindset of security service personnel.

Reflecting on my training experiences in The Gambia and Ghana, I discerned the potential pitfalls within the programs designed to shape law enforcement officers and guardians of societal well-being. A critical examination of the Gambian Police Force's history unveiled its roots, intertwined with the British colonial legacy. Established in 1816 to safeguard British interests, the force's primary objective was to impose order and maintain control, serving the colonial agenda rather than the citizens' welfare.

Post-independence, the Gambia Police Force underwent transformations, yet the training methodology and the institution's ethos remained deeply ingrained in the legacy of subservience to the ruling government. The training programs, even until recent times, were centred around loyalty to the government, particularly the president, rather than the state itself.

The recruitment practices mirrored these historical imprints. Historically, the emphasis was not on academic excellence but on physical attributes like height and strength. However, there has been a shift in recent times with the inclusion of university graduates in the police force. Although commendable, the infusion of intellectual diversity was often overshadowed by the persistent 'Us versus Them' mentality cultivated during training.

Training schools play a pivotal role in shaping personnel and the execution of their duties. However, in The Gambia, the training and practice of security have historically revolved around loyalty and patriotism to the ruling government, particularly the president, rather than a broader allegiance to the state. Despite over 165 years of existence, the recruitment and training program of the Gambia Police Force (GPF) has seen minimal changes.

During the colonial era and extending into the days of the Field Force, recruitment, particularly for lower ranks in the police force, prioritised physical attributes like height, strength, and fitness rather than academic excellence. However, amidst this, individuals of exceptional intelligence were selected, many of whom ascended the ranks to become highly accomplished officers. Surprisingly, until recently, the GPF continued to admit Grade 9 graduates into its ranks. However, there was a notable shift with the inclusion of university graduates into the cadet core, leading to a diverse pool of talents within the force.

This evolution was spurred by the visionary initiative of former Inspector General of Police Yankuba Sonko, who championed the unprecedented recruitment of university graduates and sponsored serving officers to pursue higher education. Despite occasional poor performance among some personnel, the GPF now boasts a rich human resource base, which, if effectively harnessed, could transform it into an enviable force.

Nevertheless, the GPF's training programs and facilities urgently need a significant boost. It's a universal truth that a person's environment, socialisation, and the treatment they receive profoundly influence their interactions and relationships with others. During their training, recruits were systematically stripped of their civilian identities, replacing them with the spirit and thinking of a police officer. This transformation fostered a pervasive 'them versus us' sentiment, often leading security personnel to adopt a superior attitude over civilians.

The training process, unfortunately, was marred by excessive and unnecessary punishment methods such as the infamous 'monkey dance,' 'frog jumps,' push-ups, and squats. Instructors sometimes commanded recruits to carry out irrelevant, senseless tasks, all instilling obedience to orders. The absurdity of these practices extended to instances where recruits were asked to run long distances to pluck leaves from trees or bathe fully clothed, experiences that mirrored the dehumanising treatment meted out to some arrested criminals.

Such attitudes seeped into the broader interaction of security personnel with civilians. It was common to hear derogatory terms like 'you dirty civilian' uttered by soldiers. Security personnel often approached their duties with a sense of favour, soliciting bribes and displaying minimal or no customer care. Consequently, the training and experiences of Gambian security personnel stood in stark contrast to democratic and civic-centered security values.

This misalignment was underscored by the Security Sector Reform Assessment Report of 2017, which highlighted gaps in training as a significant obstacle to reforming security institutions. The report underlines a crucial imperative: the urgent need to reorient security services within a democratic framework. This reorientation should prioritise human rights and human security, necessitating a huge shift in the training ethos.

In essence, the evolution of Gambian security institutions is at a crossroads. The rich human resources within the GPF, including a growing pool of university graduates, signify a wealth of untapped potential. A holistic revamp of training methodologies is imperative to harness this potential fully. By aligning training practices with democratic values, human rights, and civic engagement, The Gambia can nurture a security force that truly serves and protects its citizens, fostering a society where mutual respect and understanding between civilians and security personnel form the bedrock of stability and progress.

Bonds Beyond Borders: A Tale of Esprit de Corps

In 2015, amidst a peacekeeping mission in Darfur, I crossed paths with Abdou Goudiaby (Kujabi), a dedicated member of the Senegalese Formed Police Unit (FPU) stationed in Nertiti, Central Darfur, while I was deployed at the Mukjar Team Site in the same region. What began as a chance encounter evolved into a profound brotherhood and an inspiring display of camaraderie, especially when my own department left me in a challenging situation.

We met briefly when Abdou and his colleagues stopped at our team site in Mukjar, waiting for their chopper during a transit. The natural bond between Gambian and Senegalese officers, rooted in the Senegambia relationship, made it easy for my fellow Gambian police officer, Abdoulie Jallow, and me to connect with them. Furthermore, Abdou and I shared the same surname, which naturally drew us closer. Though our paths diverged after that encounter, we stayed in touch, occasionally communicating until the end of our mission.

At some point, we lost contact, but thanks to social media, specifically Facebook, we occasionally stayed in touch. In 2018, while pursuing my master's degree in the UK, Abdou's unwavering encouragement and motivation were crucial in keeping me focused on my goals.

My studies concluded in December 2019, and I eagerly anticipated returning home in April 2020. However, the rapid spread of COVID-19 across Europe led to a widespread lockdown, grounding flights, including my already booked one. Consequently, I endured an extended five-month stay in the UK, awaiting an opportunity to return.

As my approved study leave period neared its end, I informed the Office of the Inspector General of Police (IGP) about my situation. When lockdown restrictions gradually eased and flights resumed, I attempted to secure a flight home. Unfortunately, The Gambia remained under lockdown. In this trying time, a Gambian military colleague, who had also completed studies in Japan, suggested booking a flight to Dakar, Senegal, and requesting my department to arrange transportation from there. This privilege had been accorded to him by the Gambia Armed Forces, recognizing my seniority as a police officer; he reckoned that I should also get that privilege. Given that I had kept the office of the IGP informed of my situation, I assumed that it could lend me support to get home safely.

Before booking the flight to Senegal, I officially notified the IGP's office of my intention to return via Dakar and requested pickup arrangements. Regrettably, my request went unanswered. I reached out to the Personal Assistant of the IGP, who told me that my request was on the IGP's desk and promised to follow up on it and get back to me. When he did, the news was not so good; the advice was that I try to find my way home, and the office would see what it could do afterwards. I knew then if I had to make it home, I had to do so without the help of my institutions. Undeterred, I proceeded with my travel plans. Given the evolving COVID protocols, I contacted Abdou for information on Senegal's entry requirements.

To my astonishment, Abdou, a Senegalese police officer whom I had met briefly in 2015, demonstrated a level of support that my department, where I had served for eleven years, had not. Not only did Abdou provide the necessary information, but he also offered to pick me up from Dakar's airport and drive me to the Karan border. His generosity went even further as he coordinated with a colleague at the airport to expedite my immigration process.

This remarkable arrangement was made without my prior knowledge. I vividly recall the moment at the arrival lounge at 1 AM when a police officer called my name and escorted me through a swift and efficient immigration process, ensuring I was out of the airport ahead of other passengers. Waiting outside the arrival gate, Abdou greeted me warmly.

This second meeting between us in five years, marked by heavy rains that night, was a testament to the essence of esprit de corps, a bond understood by any professional security officer. Abdou's actions transcended borders, serving as a powerful reminder that, regardless of the countries we serve, individuals in the same profession are more than comrades; they are family.

Beyond the Badge: A Police Officer for Life

I returned home in the first week of September 2020 and underwent the mandatory two-week self-isolation. I then reported to the police headquarters, presenting my certificates and a letter indicating that I had completed my studies. I was given two weeks off to settle down before I resumed work. During that period, I received a letter indicating that I had been deployed as an Officer Commanding (OC) in the Community Policing Unit (CPU). I had spent most of my career in the Police, serving as a Public Relations Officer. I believed I had achieved enough and wanted to move on to something else. I had nurtured hopes that I would be deployed to the Police Training Academy, for I had a lot of ideas for reforms for the training program.

I was, however, excited I was sent to command the Community Policing Unit, which I had the privilege of overseeing for almost a year in 2015. My achievements in this position included hosting Radio and Television talk shows and other community outreach activities. Through collaboration with UNDP, I have hosted the pioneer Gambia Police Television Talk Show – "Community Policing Hour". The program delved mainly into crime in The Gambia, as well as analysis and preventive measures. I was also part of a team that compiled and published a book titled Community Policing – A Training Manual for Gambia Police Force. We also conducted several community policing training programs for both police officers and civilians across the country. We had established a network of community policing officers and volunteers. However, these gains were not consolidated and expanded upon after the end of the project. The unit had been reduced to just one personnel, ASP Lamin Badjie, who was playing the double of serving as OC Humans Rights Unit and overseeing the Community Policing Unit.

I wanted to revamp the CPU and make it a vibrant unit of the GPF, operational not only at the police headquarters but also across the country. I knew that to achieve that, I had to set up a good team. First, I developed Terms of Reference (TOR) for the Office of Community

Policing, outlining its vision, mission, and objectives. I also developed TORs for personnel serving under the unit, including the OC, administrative officer, communications and reporting officer, and gender focal person.

However, I faced the major challenge of not having an office. In fact, I had no desk to sit at, and I wondered how I could set up a team and get to work if I did not have a place to work. While I engaged the authorities to allocate me an office, I conducted interviews to select the team that would comprise the unit.

Meanwhile, just as back in 2011, when POLISO Magazine started, I was again hosted by Commissioner Ansumana Kinteh, the Commissioner of Operations. With support from ASP Lamin Badjie, I decided on the team's membership and even developed a plan for the operationalization of the unit, starting with Banjul and Kanifing Municipality. However, we made little progress beyond this owing to the lack of an office. The excitement and enthusiasm with which I started began to wane; there was not much commitment to support me in getting the unit going. During this time, I got an offer from the Food and Agriculture Organization of the United Nations, Gambia Office, to work as a Communications Officer. Applying for a leave of absence, I left to join FAO.

I worked for FAO for a year and a half and left it to join the DCAF-Geneva Centre for Security Sector Governance as a Communications Officer. Working with DCAF allowed me to work closely with the Gambia security sector to support reform. I may not wear a police uniform, but I am excited to work closely with the Police.

The life of a Gambian security officer is not for the faint of heart. It's a challenging and risky job, yet the remuneration is barely enough to sustain a decent living. Despite these odds, many young people aspire to become officers, filled with a sense of duty and a desire to serve their country with honour and integrity.

Training is rigorous and designed to instil discipline and professionalism. However, as police officers are deployed to the field, the harsh reality sets in. The lack of necessary resources, including communication and transportation facilities, makes the job more difficult. To make matters worse, many officers struggle to make ends meet due to low wages. Unsurprisingly, some officers succumb to the temptation of bribes and abuse their powers, leading to corruption within the system.

Yet, despite these challenges, many dedicated and committed officers still go above and beyond their duty to serve the country. These selfless officers are motivated by a deep love for their country and a commitment to uphold the law. Despite their meagre earnings, many officers invest their time and resources to do their jobs with distinction and positively impact their community.

The Gambia Police Force has existed for over a century, and its role in maintaining peace and stability cannot be overstated. Many officers have gone on peacekeeping missions and have been able to own a home, not because of their salary but due to the experience gained through these missions.

Despite the challenges, the Gambia Police Force remains the backbone of the country's security. From the traffic officer standing under the scorching sun on an empty stomach to the broke police officer who refuses a bribe and does their job well, these brave men and women deserve our respect and admiration.

As the Gambia strives towards security sector reform, it is essential to acknowledge and appreciate the invaluable contribution of these officers. They deserve better working conditions, pay, and resources to fulfil their duty and pridefully serve their country.

It's been thirteen years since I decided to become a police officer, and I have no regrets. The police force has significantly shaped me and made me who I am today. It's been three years since I started my leave of absence. The question remains: will I go back to the Police or not? I want to, but I am confronted with a few challenges. First, I've been stuck at the rank of superintendent of Police for eight years now, and this is so because it is a policy that one is not liable for promotion while on secondment or leave of absence.

Admittedly, some individuals have overlooked this policy, and I must note that I have been treated harshly. Before I joined FAO in December 2020, my name was on a list of officers due for promotion sent to the Personnel Management Office (PMO) for approval. The approval list returned a little after I left, and my name was scratched off the list with a pen. While I don't have qualms about this, I am upset that some officers have been promoted even while on leave of absence or secondment; in an institution like the police force, policy should be respected and applied fairly.

My colleagues are of a higher rank, and given that the Police is a hierarchical structure best enjoyed with people of the same recruitment class maintaining the same ranks, it will be a challenge for me to pick from where I left off with my contemporaries above. Furthermore, despite efforts for reform, the police force is beset with basic problems that make it hard for young officers to perform well and realise their full potential. Despite the many policies being developed and the unprecedented support for the reform process, the institution still operates under a centralised authority with uncheckered powers to make unilateral decisions with minimal or no input from others in the decision-making process.

This in itself has impeded the reform process. Security Sector Reform may be an ongoing process, but for the Gambia to fully realise the much-needed reform, it must be complemented by other transitional justice mechanisms, especially constitutional reform. It is a travesty to assume that the security sector will be fully reformed when the constitution and laws that created state-centric security institutions remain in place.

I remain a bona fide member of the Gambia Police Force. Whether I return or not, I will be eternally grateful to all who, in one way or another, helped shape this career, knowing that I will forever remain a police officer.

About the Author

David Kujabi

David Kujabi is a versatile professional, blending education, law enforcement, and communication in a career dedicated to positive societal change. With a master's degree in Peace, Conflict, and Development and a Bachelor's in English Language, he seamlessly integrates academic excellence with practical experience. Beginning as an untrained teacher, David advanced to become a vice principal before transitioning to law enforcement as a Cadet Officer in the Gambia Police Force (GPF) in 2010. Notably, he founded POLISO Magazine in 2011, showcasing his media and journalism skills. He honed his policing expertise after completing an Officers Training Course at Ghana Police College. Serving twice as a Public Relations Officer of the GPF, David excelled in shaping public perceptions. His global peacekeeping contributions include a pivotal role in Darfur and communication roles with the United Nations and DCAF. As an impassioned writer, he delves into contemporary social issues through essays and poetry, reflecting his dynamic journey from the classroom to promoting harmony in diverse settings.

www.ingramcontent.com/pod-product-compliance
Lightning Source LLC
LaVergne TN
LVHW051505170726
843492LV00002B/814